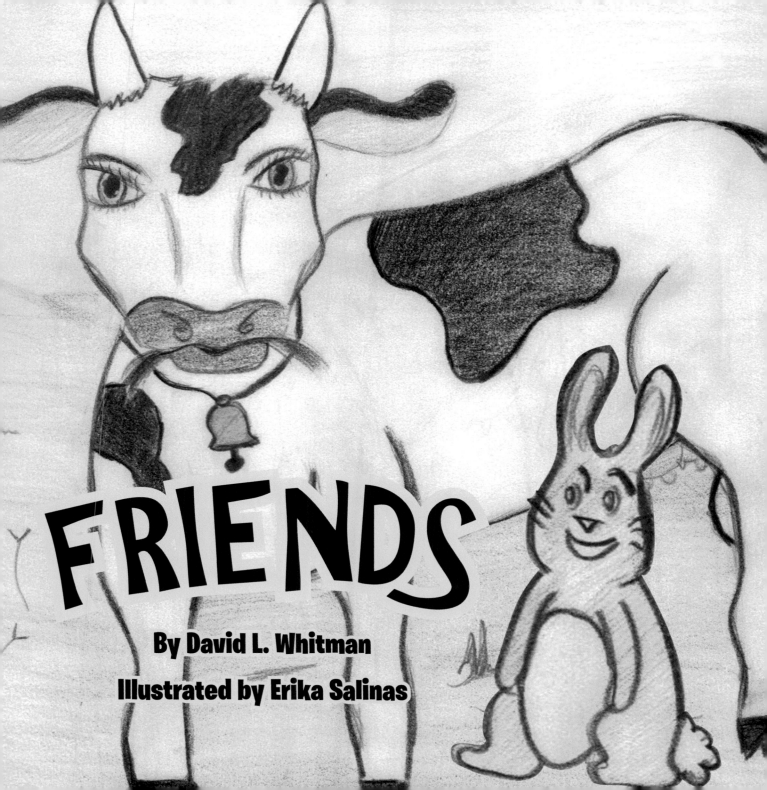

FRIENDS

By David L. Whitman

Illustrated by Erika Salinas

ISBN: 978-1-4669-6317-7

Library of Congress Control Number: 2012918985

Trafford rev. 11/27/2012

 www.trafford.com

North America & international
toll-free: 1 888 232 4444 (USA & Canada)
phone: 250 383 6864 ♦ fax: 812 355 4082

ACKNOWLEDGEMENTS:

I would like to give a big thanks to my wife, Sherri.
Also to Trafford for (you know what).

PREFACE:

When Erika was three to four years old, I got into a habit of telling her a story at bedtime. Sometimes she wanted me to tell her a real story, and sometimes she wanted me to make one up.

After making up "FRIENDS", I decided that it was good enough to write down for her. Ironically, seventeen years later, Erika illustrated it for me.

We hope you and your children will enjoy and learn from "FRIENDS".

Dedication Page:

Dedicated to my daughter, Erika, she is the one I wrote this for in the first place.

Once upon a time, in a far away land, lived a beautiful cow named "Annabelle."

1

Annabelle's home was a lovely green pasture surrounded by a strong, sturdy fence.

2

Annabelle and her two children almost always had plenty of sweet, green grass to eat.

3

As the children ate more and more grass, they grew bigger and bigger.

Until one day the grass ran out!

Annabelle was worried. She didn't know how she was going to feed her children.

5

After searching for food all day,
Annabelle finally found some grass!

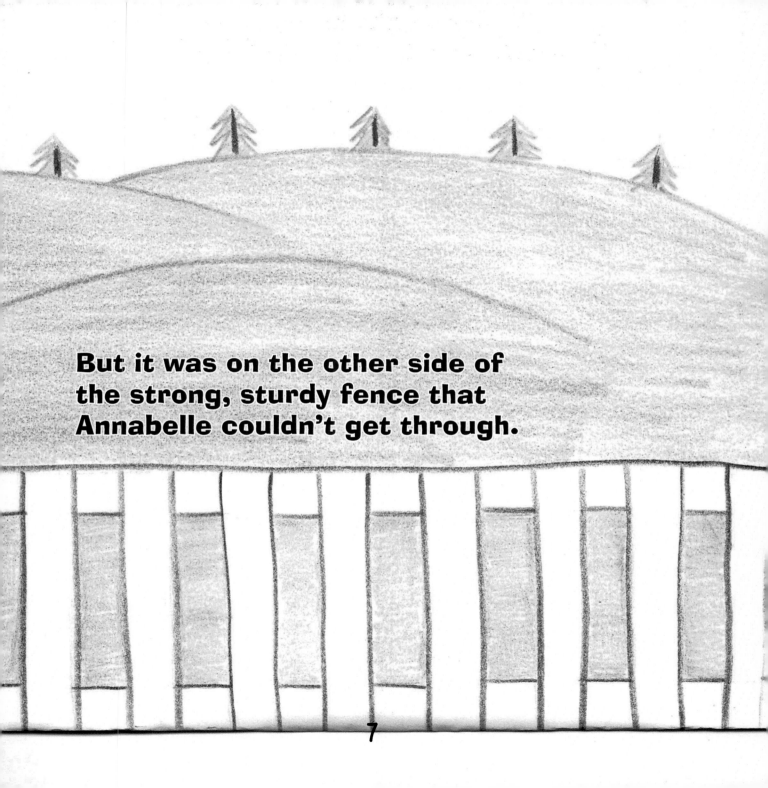

But it was on the other side of
the strong, sturdy fence that
Annabelle couldn't get through.

7

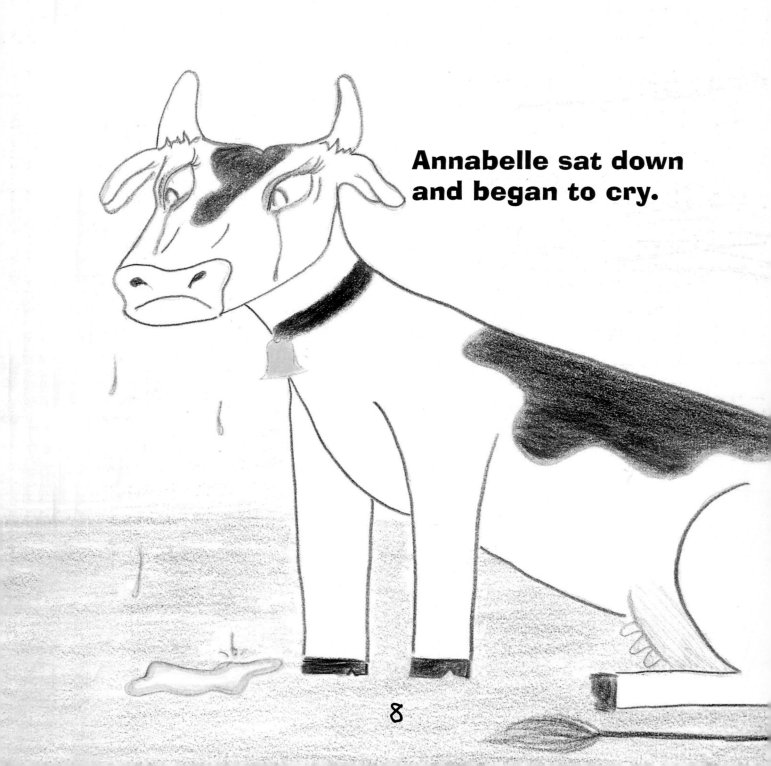

Annabelle sat down
and began to cry.

8

About that time Mr. Cotton-Tail came hopping by. He asked, Annabelle, "What's wrong?" Annabelle told Peter Cotton-Tail about the pretty green grass on the other side of the fence. Mr. Cotton-Tail said, "Annabelle, don't worry anymore" and hopped away.

Mr. Cotton-Tail went
home, got two buckets
and returned.

10

He then picked a lot of grass for Annabelle and her children.

Annabelle was so happy when Mr. Cotton-Tail gave her the grass.

11

She asked Mr. Cotton-Tail, "How can I ever thank you enough for what you have done?"

12

Mr. Cotton-Tail said, "Don't worry about it, that's what friends are for."

Later that same year it turned very cold.

By then the farmer who owned the cows was feeding them everyday. They were doing fine.

Then one night it snowed so much that the ground was completely covered.

15

The next day Mr. Cotton- Tail
couldn't find food for his family.

The only thing that he could find
was berries in Annabelle's pasture,
but he couldn't reach them.

17

Mr. Cotton-Tail was moping around in tears, when Annabelle walked up. She asked Mr. Cotton-Tail, "What's wrong?" Mr. Cotton-Tail told Annabelle the snow had all their food covered up except the berries and he couldn't reach them.

18

Annabelle said, "Mr. Cotton-Tail, don't worry anymore. I will help you get some berries to eat."

19

Annabelle told him to jump up on her back and he picked two buckets full of berries for his family.

He asked Annabelle, "How can I ever thank you enough for what you have done?"

21

Annabelle said, "Don't worry about it, that's what friends are for."

22

And be ye kind one to another, tenderhearted, forgiving one another, even as God for Christ's sake hath forgiven you.
Ephesians 4:32 KJV

The End.

Printed in the United States
By Bookmasters